S0-ARI-287

Benton Elementary School
68350 C.R. 31
Goshen, IN 46526

NATALIE SPITZER'S TURTLES

Gina Willner-Pardo
Illustrated by Molly Delaney

ALBERT WHITMAN & COMPANY
Morton Grove, Illinois

For Brian, Evan, and Cara, and for my mother. G.W-P.
For Bekah, Mima, Gabe, and Jess. M.D.

Library of Congress Cataloging-in-Publication Data

Willner-Pardo, Gina.
    Natalie Spitzer's turtles / Gina Willner-Pardo; illustrated
by Molly Delaney.
        p.   cm.
    Summary: When Jess thinks she is losing her friend Molly
to the new girl in their second-grade class, she gets interested
in Natalie Spitzer and her pet turtles.
    ISBN 0-8075-5515-0
    [1. Friendship—Fiction. 2. Schools—Fiction.
3. Turtles—Fiction.] I. Delaney, Molly, ill. II. Title.
PZ7.W68368Nat   1992
[E]—dc20   92-3342
                                                       CIP
                                                        AC

Text © 1992 by Gina Willner-Pardo.
Illustrations © 1992 by Molly Delaney.
Book design by Susan B. Cohn.
Published in 1992 by Albert Whitman & Company,
6340 Oakton Street, Morton Grove, Illinois 60053-2723.
Published simultaneously in Canada by
General Publishing, Limited, Toronto.
All rights reserved. Printed in the U.S.A.
10 9 8 7 6 5 4 3 2 1

The text for this book is set in Melior.
The illustrations are in watercolor.

Contents

1 Be Nice to Natalie!

Second grade was starting. Mom had lots of advice.

"Listen to the teacher," she said while I was brushing my teeth.

"Don't lose your book bag," she said while I was tying my shoes.

"Eat all your lunch," she said while I was having my breakfast.

"And Jess," Mom said, "be nice to Natalie Spitzer."

Uh, oh, I thought. Natalie Spitzer was the new girl from last year. She had started school in the spring, when everybody already had friends. She sat on the bench at recess. She always whispered, even outside.

"I think Natalie is lonely," Mom said. "Why don't you and Molly play with her?"

Molly Nugent was my best friend. We liked passing notes in class, hopscotch, and brownies with nuts.

"Molly and I play by ourselves," I said. "Besides, it's hard mixing old friends and new friends."

"I have lots of friends," Mom said. "It's not so hard."

Mom is very smart, I thought, slurping up my last spoonful of cereal. *But she does not know much about second grade.*

Benton Elementary
68350 C.R. 31
Goshen, IN 46526

I couldn't wait for school. I ran all three blocks.
While I was running, I thought about everything I would
tell Molly. How we had to grab desks next to each other,
like last year. How I had a new binder and a new pencil
box. How Dr. Alvarez said I was still allergic to furry
animals. No pets, she said, even though I wanted one
more than anything.

I never had a chance to tell Molly.

"Hi," she said. "There's a new girl."

I saw her. She had long, red hair, all curly down her back. Everyone was staring at her, but she didn't seem to mind. She looked as if she liked it when people paid attention to her.

"Abigail Russell," Molly said. "Isn't that a beautiful name?"

2 Everyone Loves Abigail

Second grade was starting out all wrong. Molly and I passed lots of notes. Molly wrote most of her notes about Abigail Russell.

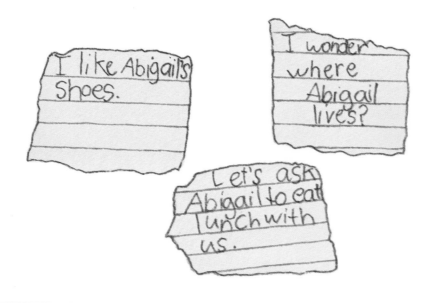

At recess, Abigail Russell ran to the swings. The second-grade girls ran behind her. Except for Natalie Spitzer. She sat on the bench.

Abigail swung higher than any of the second-grade girls.

"These swings are not as good as the ones at my old school," she said.

Abigail ran to the slide. The second-grade girls ran
behind her. Except for Natalie Spitzer.

Abigail slid faster than any of the second-grade girls.

"This slide is not as good as the one at my old school,"
she said.

"Wow," Molly said.

By the end of recess, the second-grade girls loved
Abigail Russell. Except for Natalie Spitzer.

And me.

For lunch, Abigail had chicken noodle soup in a thermos. And crackers that looked like fish. And grapes. And a brownie.

I had a peanut-butter-and-jelly sandwich and an apple.

After lunch, Abigail said, "I know a good game. Let's play horses."

"I love horses," Molly said. "How do you play?"

"Well," said Abigail, "I'll be the black horse. Black horses are fast. You can be a gray mare."

Abigail made every second-grade girl a different horse. Except for Natalie Spitzer.

And me.

"What about me?" I asked.

"I ran out of horses," Abigail said.

"I could be another gray mare," I said.

"There can only be one gray mare," Abigail said.

I looked at Molly.

"You can be the stable dog," Molly said.

"I think I'll play on the swings," I said.

3 Turtles Can't Leave You

I walked to the swings. I tried not to look at the second-grade girls.

But I could see Molly. She was busy being a gray mare.

It wasn't much fun swinging alone. I sat down on the bench next to Natalie Spitzer.

"Horses make me sneeze," Natalie whispered.

"I like dogs more anyway," I said. I thought, *Mom would like me being nice to Natalie.*

"Do you have a dog?" Natalie asked.

"Dogs make me sneeze." I remembered Dr. Alvarez, and for a second, I thought I would cry. "Do you have one?"

"No," whispered Natalie. "I have turtles."

"Turtles are dumb pets," I said.

"They are not!" Natalie wasn't whispering anymore.

"You can't pet a turtle. You can't walk a turtle. You can't give a turtle a bath," I said.

"Turtles are not like dogs and cats," Natalie said. "You have to find different ways to play with turtles."

"How many turtles do you have?" I asked.

"Three," said Natalie. "Buster, Grace, and Fluffy."

"Fluffy?"

Natalie smiled. "Not because she *is* fluffy. Because she wishes she were."

Suddenly I started to like Natalie Spitzer.

"Could I meet Fluffy sometime?" I asked.

"She's shy," Natalie said, "but she loves company."

I didn't get to meet Fluffy until Saturday, when Mom drove me to Natalie's house.

Natalie's room was wonderful. She had books about everything. Animals. Baseball. Building model airplanes.

She collected things. Shells and rocks and feathers and leaves.

And she could draw. Her pictures were hanging on every wall. She was working on a picture of a horse in a field. I thought, *Natalie Spitzer knows more about horses than Abigail Russell ever will.*

"This is where they live," Natalie said. Buster, Grace, and Fluffy were in a big glass box. I think they were just waking up.

"They look like rocks," I said.

"You have to get to know them," Natalie said. "Each one is different. Each one is special."

"What do you mean?"

"Well," Natalie said, "Buster eats flies. Grace eats worms. Fluffy likes bananas."

"Fluffy the turtle likes bananas?" I laughed.

Natalie laughed, too. "And Fluffy likes to swim. Buster and Grace like to lie in the sun."

We watched the turtles. Buster and Grace sat very still. Fluffy stretched. She made her way to the edge of the rock. Slowly, she slipped under the water.

"Turtles are different from dogs and cats," Natalie said. "They can't get lost. They can't run away. They can't leave you and find someone else to like more than you."

I thought, *It would be nice not to be left.*

"I see what you mean about turtles," I said.

"Maybe your mom would let you have one," Natalie said.

"What would it do by itself all day?" I asked.
"Wouldn't it be lonely?"

"Buster and Grace and Fluffy and I could visit,"
Natalie whispered.

"It's hard mixing old friends and new friends," I said.
"But it's worth a try."

Natalie smiled. I think Fluffy did, too.

4 The Horses Get Mad

On Monday, I passed Natalie a note.

Mom says I can have a turtle.
But I have to earn the money for one.
And for a tank and food.

Natalie wrote back:

Great! How will you earn enough money?

I wrote:

Let's think of ways at recess.

I could see Molly watching us read our notes. I think she felt the way I did when Abigail ran out of horses.

At recess, Natalie and I sat on the bench. Natalie brought a notebook and pencils. "To write down our ideas," she said.

I looked up when I heard Lucy D'Agostino and the second-grade girls.

"I want to gallop," I heard Lucy say.

"You're a foal. Foals can't gallop," Abigail said.

"But I *want* to!" Lucy said.

"Do you want to play or not?" Abigail asked.

"No, I don't!" Lucy stomped off.

The second-grade girls watched Lucy head for the slide. Some of them followed her.

Abigail looked around the playground. I could tell she was thinking. She started walking toward Natalie and me.

"Hi, Jess," Abigail said. "We need a foal." Abigail didn't even say hi to Natalie.

But being a foal sounded like fun.

"I will only play a little while," I said.

Natalie smiled, but she looked sad.

Being a foal was not as much fun as it sounded.

"You stand here," Abigail said.

"Why?" I asked.

"This is where the foal has to stand," she said.

"Why?" I asked.

"Do you want to play or not?" Abigail asked.

I looked over at Natalie. She was drawing something in our notebook.

"Jess," Molly whispered, "you have to play the way Abigail says."

"Why?" I asked.

Molly thought for a second.

"I'm not sure," she said.

5 Old Friends, New Friends

I'm going to play with Natalie," I said to Molly. "Do you want to play with us? We're thinking of ways to earn money. I'm going to buy a turtle."

"Turtles are dumb pets," Abigail said. "At my old school, nobody had turtles for pets."

Molly looked at Abigail. Then she smiled at me.

"I can make lemonade. And peanut-butter cookies. Maybe we could sell them."

"Good idea," I said. "Let's see what Natalie says."

Natalie listened to Molly's plan. "I don't like to cook," she said.

Molly put her hands on her hips. I could tell she didn't think this was going to work out.

I knew it, I thought. *Old friends and new friends just don't mix.*

"But I like to build things," Natalie said. "I could build a lemonade stand."

"And I like to paint," I said. "I could paint a sign."

I looked over at Abigail Russell. Most of the second-grade girls had gotten tired of playing horses, but a few were standing around. They were pretending to eat hay. Abigail was telling them to snort and stamp their feet. They looked bored.

Molly and Natalie were talking about what to paint on our sign. I listened to them for awhile. Molly didn't ask Natalie if she wanted to play or not. Natalie didn't tell Molly what anyone at her old school did.

I'm still not sure about mixing old friends and new friends. But I think it's worth a try.